When Lyla Got Lost

(and found)

by
Abbie Schiller
and
Samantha Kurtzman-Counter

Illustrated by
Kaori Onishi

Based on the screenplay by: Ruby Vanderzee Book Design: Deborah Keaton

My name is Lyla.
I'm six years old,
and once I got
lost.

It was a super-hot summer day, so Mama took us to the mall to keep cool.

Mama even let us pick out a treat!
I chose a yellow bouncy ball.

It bounced so high, it got away from me!

Luckily, I found it
underneath a clothes rack.

When I went to grab it, a
silly monkey hat landed on my head!

I wanted to show Mama
my funny hat.

But she wasn't
there.

That's when I knew
I was
lost.

"MAAAAA MAAAAAAAA!!!"

I yelled and hoped she would hear me.

But she didn't.

So I asked another mom for
help.

She wondered if I knew
Mama's phone number.

But I didn't.

So together, we went
to the cash register.

The saleslady said my mama's name really loud over all the speakers in the store...

...and my mama came rushing around the corner to find me!

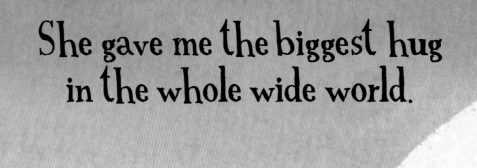

She gave me the biggest hug
in the whole wide world.

We were finally
back together again.

It sure felt good to be

found.

Lyla's tips if you ever get lost:

1. Stop right where you are and yell.

2. Ask a mom with kids for help.

3. Remember your safe adult's name and phone number.

4. Get help from a person at a cash register (if you are at a store).

5. Always stay close to your safe adult.

A note to parents and teachers

Did you know that 90% of families will experience losing a child in a public place? Getting lost ranks among the top fears for both parents and children, so being armed with the tools to manage this frightening situation is extremely important. Often parents and educators are not sure how to broach this subject without scaring children, and many are still working with outdated information. The antiquated rule for children if they ever get lost is to find a police officer - but given that police officers are rarely around and uniforms can be confusing to young children, our safety expert, Pattie Fitzgerald, recommends that a child is better off looking for a mom with kids to ask for help.

We created *When Lyla Got Lost (and found)* to arm parents, educators and children with modern, updated information. In this tale gently told through beautiful watercolor imagery, six-year-old Lyla is out shopping with her mother and little brother when she wanders off on her own. Before she knows it, she turns around and can not find her mother anywhere. Luckily for her, she remembers what to do: stop where you are and call out for your safe adult, and if that doesn't work, find a mom with kids to ask for help. She struggles to remember her mother's phone number - an important reminder to practice memorizing it with our little ones. Once Lyla is reunited with her family, she feels safe, secure, and confident knowing what to do if this ever happens again.

Here at The Mother Company we aim to instill confidence in children by giving them the tools they need to navigate tricky situations. *When Lyla Got Lost (and found)* teaches children an important lesson in a gentle, non-frightening way, empowering them to make safe and healthy choices throughout their lives.

— *Abbie Schiller & Sam Kurtzman-Counter,*
The Mother Company Mamas

With the goal of "Helping Parents Raise Good People,"
The Mother Company offers award-winning children's
books, videos, apps, activity kits, events, parenting resources
and more. Join us at TheMotherCo.com

THE MOTHER
COMPANY

HELPING PARENTS RAISE GOOD PEOPLE WITH FUN, AWARD-WINNING BOOKS & VIDEOS

The Feelings Series

"Edutainment at its best!"
— Daily Candy

The Safety Series

The Friendship Series

★★★★★
5 stars!
— Common Sense Media

SEE WHAT'S NEW AT TheMotherCo.com

INTRODUCING OUR SIBLINGS SERIES!